Happy Birthday, Anna, ¡SORPRESA!

Happy Birthday, Anna, ¡SORPRESA!

BY PATRICIA REILLY GIFF

Illustrated by DyAnne DiSalvo-Ryan

Gareth Stevens Publishing
MILWAUKEE

To Jimmy Giff, with love

For a free color catalog describing Gareth Stevens' list of high-quality books and multimedia programs, call 1-800-542-2595 (USA) or 1-800-461-9120 (Canada).
Gareth Stevens Publishing's Fax: (414) 225-0377.
See our catalog, too, on the World Wide Web: http://gsinc.com

Library of Congress Cataloging-in-Publication Data

Giff, Patricia Reilly.
    Happy birthday, Anna, ¡Sorpresa! / by Patricia Reilly Giff ;
illustrated by DyAnne DiSalvo-Ryan.
        p. cm. — (Friends and amigos)
    Summary: Sarah writes to her pen pal in South America about
her attempts to plan a surprise birthday party and her dislike of a
new girl at school.
    ISBN 0-8368-2052-5 (lib. bdg.)
    [1. Friendship—Fiction. 2. Birthdays—Fiction. 3. Pen pals—
Fiction. 4. Spanish language—Fiction.] I. DiSalvo-Ryan, DyAnne, ill.
II. Title. III. Series: Giff, Patricia Reilly. Friends and amigos.
PZ7.G3626Had   1998
[Fic]—dc21   97-40663

This edition first published in 1998 by
Gareth Stevens Publishing
1555 North RiverCenter Drive, Suite 201
Milwaukee, Wisconsin 53212 USA

Text © 1996 by Patricia Reilly Giff. Illustrations © 1996 by DyAnne DiSalvo-Ryan.
Published by arrangement with Bantam Doubleday Dell Books for Young Readers,
a division of Bantam Doubleday Dell Publishing Group, Inc., New York, New York.
All rights reserved. Additional end matter © 1998 by Gareth Stevens, Inc.

Printed in the United States of America

1 2 3 4 5 6 7 8 9 02 01 00 99 98

Where to find the Spanish Lessons in this book:

Felicidades
(feh-lee-see-DAH-dehs)

Happy Birthday

Felicidades a ti,
(feh-lee-see-
DAH-dehs ah TEE)

Happy birthday
  to you,

felicidades a ti,
(feh-lee-see-
DAH-dehs ah TEE)

Happy birthday
  to you,

felicidades, Anna,
(feh-lee-see-
DAH-dehs AH-nah)

Happy birthday,
  dear Anna,

¡felicidades a ti!
(feh-lee-see-
DAH-dehs ah TEE)

Happy birthday
  to you!

1

Feliz cumpleaños

Sarah Cole looked down at the carrot cake on her desk.

"Here goes," she whispered to her best friend, Anna.

Sarah hated carrot cake.

She tried to imagine it was chocolate. Chocolate with white icing, or fudge.

She opened her mouth and took a bite of cake.

She didn't want to hurt Mrs. Halfpenny's feelings, especially on her birthday.

Mrs. Halfpenny was the best teacher in the world.

The cake tasted like cream cheese and carrots. Horrible.

Sarah raced to the table near the window.

Mrs. Halfpenny was pouring soda.

Sarah took a quick gulp.

Outside, she could see her little sister Erica's class in the schoolyard. Erica and her friend Thomas Attonichi were looking up.

They waggled their tongues when they saw her.

Sarah waggled her tongue, too, before she went back to her seat.

The classroom looked different today. Mrs. Halfpenny had changed seats this morning.

Anna was sitting on one side of her.

Tuesday Thompson was on the other.

Just her luck.

Tuesday was a pain sometimes.

Right now no one was sitting. Everyone

was running around. And the classroom was noisy. Noisier than she had ever heard it.

Benjamin Bean had climbed up on the computer table.

He was batting a balloon up toward the ceiling.

Sarah tiptoed toward him.

"Watch out, Benjamin!" Tuesday yelled before Sarah could hit the balloon.

"Hey," Sarah said.

" 'Happy Birthday . . . ,' " someone started to sing.

Sarah began to sing, too. She sang in Spanish, " *'Felicidades . . .'* "

Anna's cousin Luisa had taught it to her. Luisa was back in South America now. She had promised to be Sarah's pen pal. Sarah was waiting for her first letter.

Right now Tuesday leaned over. "I can sing 'Happy Birthday' in Italian," she said.

"My grandmother told me how."

Tuesday tossed her head around.

She had a million beads in her hair.

"Anna's birthday is in February, too," Tuesday said.

Sarah nodded. "No party, though. Anna's mother broke her ankle."

"I know." Tuesday shook her head. A purple bead flew off her braid. It bounced across the desk. "Maybe my mother will give her a party."

Tuesday sneaked a look at Anna.

Anna was on her way out the door with the girls' room pass. "A surprise party," Tuesday whispered.

Sarah bit her lip. Too bad she hadn't thought of that.

"Anna's my best friend," she said slowly.

Then she remembered. She couldn't have a party for Anna.

February was her mother's busiest month at the bakery.

She'd be icing pink Valentine cookies and baking Abraham Lincoln log cabin cakes.

She'd be dotting cherries on George Washington cupcakes.

Tuesday pulled a pad out of her desk.

She picked up a pointy pencil.

"Let me see." She frowned. "A lot of people are in the class. I might have to leave a few out."

"I'm Anna's best friend," Sarah said again quickly.

Tuesday shook her head. "I think the kids on my block have to come first."

"Never mind." Sarah stared out the window. Tuesday lived eight blocks away. "I'm having the party for Anna."

"Maybe I should be invited first," Tuesday said. "It was my idea."

Sarah narrowed her eyes.

Then she remembered.

Her mother would make her invite everyone, anyway.

"I guess so," she said. "Everyone's invited."

Tuesday stood up. "Listen, everyone. Sarah Cole is having a surprise party for Anna. The whole class is invited."

"Nice," said Mrs. Halfpenny.

"You too," Sarah told the teacher.

Then she opened her eyes wide.

How could she have forgotten her mother's busiest month?

Her mother could never do a birthday party.

And now twenty people were coming.

"*Caramba,*" she said.

It was Anna's cousin Luisa's favorite word.

A LETTER FROM SOUTH AMERICA

Querida Sarah:

Remember me? Luisa, la prima de Anna? Anna's cousin.

I am your new amiga.

Your new Spanish pen pal.

I have another pen pal. She is in Springfield Gardens too.

Her name is Martes.

Besos, XXXXX
Luisa

A LETTER FROM SPRINGFIELD GARDENS

Dear Luisa:

¿Cómo estás?

I am trying to learn one Spanish word every day.

Yesterday was cumpleaños . . . birthday.

Today is dificultad . . . trouble.

I am in dificultades.

Muchas dificultades.

It's about Anna's cumpleaños.

Besos, XXXXX
Sarah

P.S. Who is Martes? Does she go to our school?

2

Ayudar

When the bell rang, Sarah didn't wait for anything.

She rushed home and threw her books on the chair.

"Hello and good-bye," she told Aunt Minna, the baby-sitter. "I've got to talk to my mother at the bakery."

Aunt Minna was sewing a button. She snipped off the thread with her teeth.

"I just drove Erica to the bakery," Aunt Minna said. "I think your mother may have a surprise for you."

Sarah hurried down the street toward Higby Avenue.

She crossed her fingers.

Maybe her mother wouldn't mind having a birthday party.

She'd tell her mother she'd help.

Help at the bakery.

Help at home.

Help with the party.

Ayudar. A new Spanish word. Help.

Sarah pushed open the bakery door.

It smelled like pie . . . apple pie with raisins and cinnamon.

Her mother was waiting on a line of customers.

Sarah ducked behind the counter. She gave her mother a quick kiss before she went into the back.

Mannie, the baker, was rolling out rounds of dough . . . one after the other.

He put his head to one side. "*Listo . . .
done,*" he said, staring at the ovens.

He opened the doors and took out the
pies on long paddles.

Erica, Sarah's little sister, was sitting under the table. She stuck out her head. "*Hola,*
Sarah. I'm making my own pie."

Sarah looked at it.

It was the size of a fist, and filthy.

"Lovely," Sarah said. She sat down at one
end of the table.

She watched Mannie while she waited for
her mother.

Now he was dropping strawberries inside
each circle of dough. "*Fresas,*" he called the
strawberries.

Once in a while he raised his eyebrows at
Sarah and smiled.

She tried to think of what she would say
to her mother.

At last her mother bustled into the back. "Whew," she said. "It's been one of the busiest days of the—"

Sarah closed her eyes for a moment. "Listen—" she began.

Her mother held up her hand. "Me first. I have the best news."

"I know it already," Erica said from under the table.

Sarah's mother took a breath. "Daddy and I are going away. Aunt Minna, too."

"But it's the busiest time," Sarah said.

"I know it." Her mother was nodding. "Lincoln log cakes. Washington cupcakes with cherries—" She broke off. "But you're not going to believe—"

Erica stuck her head out from under the table. "Mom and Aunt Minna won third prize at the Bakery Association."

"Our secret recipe for coffee cake," said

her mother. "Remember, I dropped the coffee in by mistake."

"And then Aunt Minna dropped in the tomato soup," Sarah finished for her.

"Daddy sent it in to the contest. He called it Imagination Cake."

"Everyone loves it but me," said Erica. "And now they won a trip to Florida. They're going to close the store for three weeks." She stopped for a breath.

"Anna's birthday is coming," Sarah said.

Her mother swooped down. She put her arms around Sarah. "I know it. And Anna's mother has a broken—"

She took an edge of pie crust and popped it into Sarah's mouth. "When we get home, we'll bake Anna the most beautiful—"

"Who's going to baby-sit?" Sarah asked. Maybe someone else could do the birthday party. Maybe someone else could help.

Erica slid out from under the table. Her teeth were covered with pie crust dough. She looked worried. "That's what I want to know," she said. "Who *is* going to baby-sit?"

Their mother smiled. "Señora Sanchez."

Sarah blinked. "The lady from Benjamin's apartment?"

Señora Sanchez was an artist.

In two seconds she could draw the most beautiful pictures.

She had just come from Ecuador to live.

Sarah's mother was nodding, looking happy. "Señora Sanchez loves children. She loves dogs. Gus will have a wonderful time."

Sarah leaned back against the wall. "Señora Sanchez doesn't speak a word of English."

"Yes she does," said Erica. "Four words.

Dog, pretty, Christmas, and . . ." She frowned. "I forget the last one."

Sarah swallowed. "It doesn't make any difference," she said.

"Don't worry about Señora Sanchez's English," said her mother. "She's a terrific person. She'll take care of you perfectly. And Benjamin's mother isn't far."

"Don't worry," Erica said. "I'll teach her English."

Sarah tried to smile at her mother.

She didn't feel like smiling, though. She'd never have that birthday party now.

A LETTER FROM SOUTH AMERICA

Dear Sarah:

Martes is a nice girl. I met her at the park.

She told me a girl in her class is fresh.

Martes is sad. Triste. She wants to be her amiga.

I told her:

Be agradable . . . agreeable.

Be amistosa . . . friendly.

Be simpática . . . very nice.

How do you think?

Abrazos, OOO
Luisa

A LETTER FROM SPRINGFIELD GARDENS

Dear Luisa:

Lo siento I haven't answered your letter sooner.

A lady from Ecuador is coming to take care of us.

Your friend Martes sounds simpática.

Maybe her friend isn't so hot.

School was loco today. Crazy.

This kid Tuesday asked Anna over to her house yesterday. She didn't ask me.

Anna said it was because she didn't see me.

I think it was because she didn't want to.

She's just like Martes's friend. Malo. Mean.

Besos, XXXX
Sarah

3

Señora Sanchez

Everyone was at the front door, waving. Sarah, Erica, Anna, and Señora Sanchez.

Even skinny Thomas Attonichi from down the street.

Gus, their huge yellow dog, was barking and racing around the lawn.

Bonita, Señora Sanchez's dog, was chasing him. She bounced around like a tennis ball . . . and she was just about that size.

Gus looked worried, though. With his eyes rolled back, he dashed away from her.

Benjamin was laughing, holding on to his

puppy, Perro. "Don't be afraid, Gus," he called.

It was hard to hear.

Erica was down on the bottom step, crying, screeching. "Suppose you never come back!" she called to their mother.

Their mother rolled the window down and blew kisses at them. "Of course we're coming—"

Their father tooted the horn as he backed out of the driveway.

The car turned the corner before Sarah could hear the rest of what their mother was saying.

Besides, Erica was making so much noise, no one could hear anything.

Señora Sanchez put her hand on Sarah's shoulder. *"Galletas y leche,"* she said.

Sarah tried to think. *Y* was "and." But what was *galletas*? What was *leche*?

It was almost as bad as Luisa's letter with all those words. *Agradable* and *amistosa,* and *simpática.*

Erica poked her head up. She smiled at Señora Sanchez. "Cookies," she said. "Cookies and milk."

Señora Sanchez looked around at everyone and smiled, too. The little bells on her earrings made tinkling sounds. "Kitchen," she said.

"Good," Erica said. "That's a new word in English."

Señora Sanchez held up her hand. "Five words," she said.

"Yes," said Erica, sliding off the steps. "Let's study English. We'll make lists all over the place."

Señora Sanchez scooped up Bonita. "*Muy bien.* Good."

Sarah ran for Gus.

Everyone else was trooping into the house.

Then Sarah saw Tuesday.

She was coming down the street.

She must be on her way to Anna's house.

Too bad. Anna was inside her house.

Sarah closed her eyes and backed up the steps to her house.

Then she raced inside and slammed the door.

She could hear Señora Sanchez saying, "*Listos. Galletas y leche.*"

Listos. They're ready, Sarah thought.

She thought she heard something else, too.

Tuesday calling her name.

Maybe not.

Sarah went down the hall and into the kitchen.

SEÑORA SANCHEZ'S ENGLISH LESSONS

 rain   lluvia
(YOO-vyah)

 snow   nieve
(NYEH-veh)

sun   sol
(SOHL)

 cloud   nube
(NOO-beh)

4

Escoba

It was Monday morning. Sarah had been thinking of Anna's birthday party all weekend.

Talking to herself about it.

"What are you saying?" Erica kept asking.

"Stop following me around," Sarah kept answering.

Right now it was almost time for school.

Maybe she could get Señora Sanchez to help, Sarah thought for the hundredth time.

Why not? She pulled on her socks.

She'd ask her at breakfast.

Señora Sanchez had learned a bunch of words in English this weekend. Sarah had heard her singing, "*Sábado* is Saturday. *Domingo* is Sunday.*" At the same time she was painting a picture of Gus and Bonita chasing each other.

But how could Sarah make Señora Sanchez understand the whole thing? Inviting the whole class to a birthday party . . . without asking her mother . . .

Sarah had learned only one new word in Spanish. *Angel.*

That's what Señora Sanchez called her. *Angel.* And that word wouldn't help one bit.

Sarah was going to be late for school. There was no time to try to make Señora Sanchez understand.

Sarah had to smile. Last night Señora Sanchez had dropped the alarm clock.

The hands had fallen off, and the alarm had rung every hour until the middle of the night.

Then it had stopped . . . probably forever.

Sarah went down to the kitchen.

Señora Sanchez was standing on a chair.

She was painting tiny birds and flowers on the wall above the door.

Benjamin had told Sarah that Señora Sanchez had been a famous artist in Ecuador.

Sarah looked up at a small yellow bird with its wings spread. Then she smelled something. "Look!" she yelled.

Pancakes were burning on the griddle.

Señora Sanchez jumped off the chair. She knocked a box of pancake flour on the floor. "*¡Qué barbaridad!*" she said.

She shoved the griddle to the back of the

stove. "Hot," she said, and snapped her fingers. "*Escoba,* please."

Sarah looked around the kitchen. *Escoba . . . escoba . . .*

She held up the dishtowel.

Señora Sanchez shook her head.

Her bell earrings jingled.

Smoke was still coming from the pancake griddle.

Señora Sanchez waved her hand at it. "*Un minuto,*" she said.

Erica giggled. "Black pancakes for breakfast."

Señora Sanchez reached for a pad and pencil. She drew a broom with long curly bristles. "*Escoba,*" she said.

"Broom," said Sarah.

"Brum," said Señora Sanchez. "*Sí.*"

Sarah watched Señora Sanchez reaching for the pancake turner.

"*¡Qué barbaridad!*" Señora Sanchez said again.

The pancakes were cemented to the griddle.

Señora Sanchez made clicking noises with her tongue.

She dumped the griddle into the sink. It sizzled on top of last night's dishes.

Señora Sanchez reached for a box of cereal.

"Cornflakes," she said.

"A new word," said Erica. "*Bueno.*"

Sarah poured milk onto her cereal.

She looked at Señora Sanchez. "Anna's *cumpleaños* . . . ," she began.

But Señora Sanchez had started on their lunch bags.

"*Jamón,*" she said, making the sloppiest ham sandwich Sarah had ever seen.

Lettuce and tomatoes were hanging out the edges.

Señora Sanchez was listening, though.

"Cumpleaños," she said. *"Anna, simpática."*

Sarah had heard that word before. She had read it in Luisa's letter.

"What does . . . ," she began, and stopped.

Señora Sanchez might not be able to tell her, anyway.

She watched Señora Sanchez stuffing the sandwiches into enough foil to wrap the whole kitchen, and thought about the birthday party.

The kitchen was a mess . . . her new word, *sucia.*

So was the rest of the house.

How could they ever get it fixed in time?

How could she even make Señora Sanchez understand?

In the living room, the clock was chiming.

Good grief. Nine o'clock.

She was late . . . really late.

She grabbed her jacket and raced out the
door.

A LETTER FROM SOUTH AMERICA

Dear Sarah:

I had a carta from Martes. She says she tries to be amistosa.

This girl with brown hair and long face is not amistosa back. Everyone goes to Long Face's house. They do not ask Martes to come.

Long Face closes the door in her face.

Cariños,
Luisa

P.D. What is happening with Anna's cumpleaños?

A LETTER FROM SPRINGFIELD GARDENS

Dear Luisa:

No time to write.

Everything is going wrong since my mother went away.

Señora Sanchez has broken the washing machine, the dryer, and she can't cook.

The cumpleaños es un gran problema.

Cuatro besos, XXXX
Sarah

P.S. Señora Sanchez has painted a gorgeous picture of Anna.

~~~~~~~~~~~~~~~~~~~~~~~~~~~~~~

5

Un fantasma

It was recess time. Large white flakes of snow were blowing across the schoolyard.

Mrs. Halfpenny took them outside anyway.

Sarah held her face up to catch the flakes.

She thought of her mother and father and Aunt Minna.

It seemed as if they had been gone forever.

Last night they had called. "Just another couple of days," her mother had said.

It was hard for Sarah to pay attention, though.

Bonita had been jumping around the kitchen. She'd been pulling on Gus's tail.

It was the only part of him that stuck out. He'd been hiding under the table.

Right now Mrs. Halfpenny clapped her hands. "Anyone want to play Duck Duck Goose?" she called.

A bunch of kids ran to make a circle around her.

Sarah and Anna didn't, though. They ran to the inside corner of the building. There was no wind, and steam was coming up from the cafeteria window.

It smelled like pizza.

Someone was coming around the corner.

In the snow it was hard to see.

"It's a *fantasma*," Anna said. "A ghost."

"It's Benjamin Bean." Sarah smiled.

Benjamin's hat was pulled down over his

eyes. There was a hole on top where the pom-pom belonged.

Benjamin was a mess. He was a *simpático* mess, though. This morning he had stopped in before school.

He had brought a bag of homemade cookies from his mother.

Sarah had to smile.

Benjamin must know what a terrible cook Señora Sanchez was.

Sarah watched him race away.

"Teach me some words," she said to Anna. "Something I can tell Señora San-chez."

Anna looked up at the sky. A snow-flake landed on her nose. "Let's see . . . words," she said. "How about *importante*?"

"Easy," Sarah said. "Important."

"*Inmediatamente* . . ."

Sarah nodded. "It sounds like . . ."

". . . Immediately," said Anna.

They stamped their feet to keep warm.

"*Apresúrate* means 'hurry,' " Anna said.

Sarah bit her lip. "That's a good one. We've been late every day since Señora Sanchez came.

"How do you say 'party'?" she asked, without looking at Anna.

" 'Party'?" Anna leaned over to see into the cafeteria window. "They're making salad to go with the pizza."

"Too bad," Sarah said. "I've got a sloppy ham sandwich."

Just then Tuesday rushed by. She was bouncing a ball against the side of the building.

She whispered to Sarah in between the bounces. "I didn't forget about Saturday."

Sarah swallowed. She wondered if Anna had heard.

Anna watched Tuesday reach the end of the building. "What's Saturday?" she asked. "Besides my birthday?"

Sarah felt her face get hot. "I don't know."

That Tuesday was such a pest.

She was even learning Spanish . . . probably just because Sarah was.

Sarah had seen a piece of paper on her desk. It had said *"amistosa . . . ,"* and something else.

Sarah hadn't seen the rest.

Tuesday had swept it up. She had stuck it in her pocket.

Anna didn't say anything for a long moment.

They leaned against the window as the cafeteria lady rushed along the table. She was dropping a couple of olives into each salad.

Then Anna began again. "Saturday . . . *sábado.*"

Sarah wanted to say she knew that one.

She didn't, though.

"Sunday is *domingo,*" Anna said. She spoke softly, slowly.

She kept looking toward Tuesday at the end of the building.

Sarah knew what she was thinking.

She was thinking about Sarah and Tuesday doing something without her.

She was thinking about being left out.

Sarah wanted to say something.

If only she could tell her about Mrs. Halfpenny marking the calendar . . . and the whole class coming for a surprise party.

Sarah swallowed. The party she couldn't even have.

"*Fiesta,*" Anna said suddenly.

Sarah blinked. "What?"

"You asked the word for 'party.' It's *fiesta.*"

"Of course. I forgot." Sarah sighed. *Fiesta.*

A LETTER FROM SOUTH AMERICA

Querida Sarah:

I have had dos cartas this week.
Una from you.
Una from Martes.
I hope you are happy . . . feliz.
Martes is triste . . . sad.
Long Face will not be her amiga. She does not talk to her.
Too bad you do not know Martes. You could be amigas.

Besos,
Luisa

6

¿Qué?

It was dark outside, suppertime.

Sarah could smell something cooking.

It smelled like cough drops.

She went into the kitchen and sniffed.

Señora Sanchez was sitting at the table with Erica.

She looked up when she saw Sarah. "*¿Qué?*"

"That means 'What?' " said Erica.

"What's that horrible smell?" Sarah asked.

"*¿Qué?*" Señora Sanchez asked again.

Erica waved her hand. "Be quiet, Sarah,

please. I'm giving Señora Sanchez her English lesson."

Sarah lifted the pot cover.

Behind her Erica was talking in a loud voice. "I made a picture. It's Benjamin Bean. He's a boy. And me, Erica. I'm a girl."

Inside the pot was a horrible mess of something green . . . spinach, probably. But there was something else, too. Little pieces of mushrooms.

They'd been in the refrigerator, left over since Christmas.

Sarah opened her mouth.

But Señora Sanchez and Erica weren't paying attention.

Señora Sanchez was snapping her fingers. She was singing. *"Niño es* boy. *Niña es Erica."*

Sarah could see the bottom of the pot.

It was black.

Sizzling.

Burning.

"The spinach," she told Señora Sanchez, and pointed.

"*¡Ay, ay, ay, ayyy!*" yelled Señora Sanchez.

She dashed for the pot and pulled it away from the oven.

She looked down at the spinach. "*Pobrecitas,*" she said.

Erica was laughing. "That means 'poor little things,'" she said. "She means the spinach."

"*Espinacas,*" said Señora Sanchez.

"That means—" Erica began.

"I can guess," said Sarah. "'Spinach.'"

"Oh, well," Señora Sanchez said, looking at the pot.

"I taught her that," said Erica. "*Muy bien,*" she told Señora Sanchez.

Señora Sanchez sat down at the table again. She was singing the McDonald's song.

"I can guess what that means, too," Sarah said. "We're having McDonald's tonight."

"Shh. We're studying now." Erica turned to Señora Sanchez. "Today is Monday."

She said it in a voice that could be heard down the street.

"*Lunes*," Señora Sanchez said, in a loud voice, too. "Today is Monday."

"*Muy bien*," said Erica. "Tomorrow is Tuesday."

"*Sí*. Tomorrow is Tuesday," Señora Sanchez shouted. "*Martes.*"

Sarah felt her throat go dry. "What?" she asked.

Erica and Señora Sanchez looked up at her.

"*¿Qué?*" Señora Sanchez asked.

Sarah sank down in a chair.

"Tomorrow is Tuesday," Erica said. "You didn't know that?"

"*Martes,*" said Sarah slowly.

She couldn't believe it.

She half-listened as Erica began again.

They were doing food now.

"Carrots," said Erica, drawing a fat orange lump.

"*Zanahorias,*" sang Señora Sanchez.

Tuesday was *martes,* Sarah thought. And *martes* was Tuesday.

Could that be?

Erica drew a purple circle. "Beets."

"*Ah,*" said Señora Sanchez. "*Remolachas.*"

Sarah thought back to Luisa's letters: Martes came from Springfield Gardens, Luisa had said. "I met her at the park."

The park on Higby Avenue . . . two blocks from the bakery?

And the scrap of paper on Tuesday's desk. *Amistosa.*

Tuesday was learning Spanish.

"Tomatoes," Erica said, working with a red crayon.

"*Tomates,*" said Señora Sanchez.

Sarah sat there for a moment. "Is my face long?" she asked Erica, her voice sounding strange.

Erica put her head on one side. "I guess so. It's like that horse picture hanging in the hall."

Sarah ran her tongue over her lips.

"But don't worry," Erica said. She picked up a brown crayon. "I love horses."

Sarah didn't answer. She looked out the window at the darkness.

How terrible.

She was Long Face.

SEÑORA SANCHEZ'S ENGLISH LESSONS

 spinach espinacas
(ehs-pee-NAH-kahs)

 carrot zanahoria
(sah-nah-OH-ryah)

 beet remolacha
(reh-moh-LAH-chah)

 tomato tomate
(toh-MAH-teh)

 horse caballo
(kah-BAH-yoh)

7

Martes

It was Friday, after school.

Everyone was kneeling in front of the couch. Señora Sanchez, Erica, and Sarah. And even Benjamin and Tuesday.

Gus, the dog, was wedged underneath.

He had crawled under to get away from Bonita.

Bonita was having a wonderful time, jumping around on the couch pillows. So was Benjamin's dog, Perro.

"Come on, Gus," Sarah said.

The dog didn't move.

"Never mind." Erica shook her head. "He's such a coward."

"I guess he'll come out when he's ready," Sarah said.

She smiled at Tuesday.

Tuesday had turned out to be a surprise this week.

Not a pain, after all.

Yes, she had met Luisa in the park.

Yes, she was writing to Luisa, too.

And yes, she'd love to help Sarah with the party.

In fact, what they were going to do right now was Tuesday's idea.

They went into the kitchen. All of them except Gus.

Bonita was up on the kitchen table in an instant . . . yanking at the flowers in the yellow bowl.

Señora Sanchez's head was turned to one side. *"¿Qué?"* she asked.

"We want to have a party for Anna," Sarah said. "Tomorrow."

"Muy bien," said Señora Sanchez. She was nodding . . . all set to do whatever they wanted.

"Fiesta," Tuesday said.

"Ah," said Señora Sanchez.

"Start to draw," Tuesday told Erica.

Erica pulled paper and crayons from the drawer. "I'm good at this," she said.

"Muy buena," said Sarah.

"Fiesta for Anna," Benjamin said.

He looked at the pots in the sink. *"Muy* messy," he said, grinning.

"How about drawing a cake?" Tuesday asked.

"With candles," Sarah said.

"And presents," said Benjamin.

"And party hats," said Tuesday.

"Good thing I'm a terrific artist," said Erica.

Señora Sanchez was watching Erica draw. Before Erica finished, she began to help. In a moment there was a picture of Anna in a party hat, and a cake with tiny candles.

"Torta," Señora Sanchez told them. *"Candelas. Regalos. Sí."*

She gave Erica a hug. *"Sí. Fiesta."*

She looked around the kitchen and yelled, "Messy!"

"I taught her that," Erica told Benjamin.

Señora Sanchez rolled up her sleeves.

She began to sing . . . slowly. "No mess for *la fiesta!*"

A LETTER FROM ERICA

Querida Luisa:

Sarah es tu amiga por correspondencia.

Martes es tu amiga por correspondencia.

Quiero ser tu amiga por correspondencia.

XXX OOO
Erica

P.S. Anna's fiesta is mañana.

P.S. Señora Sanchez helped me write this.

Una sorpresa

Everyone was in the living room: the whole class, even Mrs. Halfpenny.

Mrs. Halfpenny had brought carrot cake with cream cheese icing.

It was a good thing.

The cake that Sarah and Tuesday and Señora Sanchez had made was *muy malo*!

Sarah peeked out the window.

She could see Anna starting through the woods.

"Anna is coming," Sarah told Señora Sanchez. She shook her head. It was hard to remember to say things in Spanish. *"Anna viene."*

Señora Sanchez was humming. She was drying the last pot. "Anna is coming," she sang.

Sarah couldn't wait until Anna got to this side of the woods.

She thought back to the schoolyard the other day.

She didn't want Anna to feel left out.

She looked down at the plate of candy on the table. *Los dulces.* And the balloons on the ceiling. *Globos.*

Then she heard it. Anna yelling. "Sarah? Did you call me on the phone? My mother said you were—"

Sarah didn't wait to hear the rest.

She pulled open the door.

"¡Sorpresa, Anna!" she called.

A moment later everyone else was yelling, too.

And Anna was smiling, laughing. She began to rip open packages a mile a minute.

Sarah had gone out with Señora Sanchez and Erica last night. They had found writing paper and candy.

They had even stopped at Señora's apartment for a pretty pin for Anna.

Right now wrapping paper was on the floor.

Anna was holding up the beautiful painting that Señora Sanchez had made of her.

Benjamin was throwing peanuts up in the air.

He was trying to make Perro catch them.

But Perro didn't care about the peanuts. He was trying to grab a piece of cake from the table.

And Señora Sanchez was singing, teaching everyone to dance.

Then she stopped.

She hugged Sarah and Erica. *"Feliz,"* she said.

"Happy," said Sarah. *"Sí."*

"Más sorpresas," Señora said. She pointed to the window.

At first Sarah didn't see anything . . . just the snow on the curb, and the postman going up the street.

Erica saw it first.

The blue car piled high with luggage.

Her mother and father. Home.

Sarah didn't wait for her coat and boots.

She raced outside, waving. "Welcome home!" she yelled.

"Yes," Señora called. *"Bienvenidos."*

A LETTER FROM SPRINGFIELD GARDENS

Dear Luisa:

I met Martes.
She's agradable.
She's amistosa.
She's simpática.
Anna's cumpleaños is over. Mine is next.
I think Anna and Martes are going to have a fiesta sorpresa for me!

Besos, XXXX
Sarah

Glossary

....

a *(AH)*	to
abrazo *(ah-BRAH-soh)*	hug
agradable *(ah-grah-DAH-bleh)*	agreeable
ah *(AH)*	oh
amiga *(ah-MEE-gah)*	friend (a girl)
amiga por correspondencia *(ah-MEE-gah pohr* *coh-rrehs-pohn-DEHN-syah)*	pen pal
amigas *(ah-MEE-gahs)*	friends (girls)
amistosa *(ah-mees-TOH-sah)*	friendly
ángel *(AHN-hehl)*	angel

apresúrate *(ah-preh-SOO-rah-teh)*	hurry up
ayudar *(ah-yoo-DAHR)*	help, be helpful
besos *(BEH-sohs)*	kisses
¡Bienvenidos! *(byehn-veh-NEE-dohs)*	Welcome! Welcome home!
bueno *(BWEH-noh)*	good
caballo *(kah-BAH-yoh)*	horse
candelas *(kahn-DEH-lahs)*	candles
¡Caramba! *(kah-RAHM-bah)*	Wow!
Cariños, *(kah-REE-nyohs)*	Love,
carta *(KAHR-tah)*	letter
¿Cómo estás? *(KOH-moh ehs-TAHS)*	How are you?

cuatro *(KWAH-troh)*	four
cumpleaños *(koom-pleh-AH-nyohs)*	birthday
de *(DEH)*	of
dificultad(es) *(dee-fee-kool-TAHD)* *(TAH-dehs)*	difficulty, difficulties
domingo *(doh-MEEN-goh)*	Sunday
dos *(DOHS)*	two
dulces *(DOOL-sehs)*	candy (sweets)
el *(EHL)*	the (masculine singular)
es *(EHS)*	(she, he, it) is
escoba *(ehs-KOH-bah)*	broom
escuela *(ehs-KWEH-lah)*	school

español *(ehs-pah-NYOHL)*	Spanish
espinacas *(ehs-pee-NAH-kahs)*	spinach
fantasma *(fahn-TAHS-mah)*	ghost
Felicidades. *(feh-lee-see-DAH-dehs)*	Congratulations. Happy birthday.
feliz *(feh-LEES)*	happy
Feliz cumpleaños. *(feh-LEES koom-pleh-* *AH-nyohs)*	Happy birthday.
fiesta *(FYEHS-tah)*	party
fiesta sorpresa *(FYEHS-tah sohr-PREH-sah)*	surprise party
fresas *(FREH-sahs)*	strawberries
galletas *(gah-YEH-tahs)*	cookies, crackers

globos *(GLOH-bohs)*	balloons
gran, grande *(GRAHN, GRAHN-deh)*	big
hablo *(AH-bloh)*	I speak
hablo español *(AH-bloh ehs-pah-NYOHL)*	I speak Spanish
importante *(eem-pohr-TAHN-teh)*	important
inmediatamente *(een-meh-dyah-tah-MEHN-teh)*	immediately
jamón *(hah-MOHN)*	ham
la *(LAH)*	the (feminine singular)
leche *(LEH-cheh)*	milk
listo *(LEES-toh)*	ready, done
listos *(LEES-tohs)*	(they are) ready

lluvia *(YOO-vyah)*	rain
loco *(LOH-koh)*	crazy
lo siento *(loh SYEHN-toh)*	I'm sorry
los *(LOHS)*	the (masculine plural)
lunes *(LOO-nehs)*	Monday
malo *(MAH-loh)*	bad, mean
mañana *(mah-NYAH-nah)*	tomorrow
martes *(MAHR-tehs)*	Tuesday
más *(MAHS)*	more
minuto *(mee-NOO-toh)*	minute (see ``un minuto'')
mucho *(MOO-choh)*	much, a lot

muchos *(MOO-chohs)*	many
muy *(MOOEE)*	very
muy bien *(MOOEE BYEHN)*	very well very good
muy buena *(MOOEE BWEH-nah)*	very good
muy malo *(MOOEE MAH-loh)*	very bad
nieve *(NYEH-veh)*	snow
niña *(NEE-nyah)*	girl
niño *(NEE-nyoh)*	boy
nube *(NOO-beh)*	cloud
P.D., posdata *(PEH DEH, pohs-DAH-tah)*	P.S., postscript
pobrecitas *(poh-breh-SEE-tahs)*	poor little things

poco *(POH-koh)*	a little
prima *(PREE-mah)*	girl cousin
primo *(PREE-moh)*	boy cousin
problema *(proh-BLEH-mah)*	problem
¿Qué? *(KEH)*	What?
¡Qué barbaridad! *(KEH bahr-bah-ree-DAHD)*	Wow!
Querida . . . , *(Keh-REE-dah)*	Dear . . . ,
Quiero ser . . . *(KYEH-roh SEHR)*	I want to be . . .
regalos *(reh-GAH-lohs)*	presents
remolachas *(reh-moh-LAH-chahs)*	beets
sábado *(SAH-bah-doh)*	Saturday

señora *(seh-NYOH-rah)*	Mrs.
sí *(SEE)*	yes
simpática *(seem-PAH-tee-kah)*	very nice (she is)
simpático *(seem-PAH-tee-koh)*	very nice (he is)
sol *(SOHL)*	sun
sorpresa *(sohr-PREH-sah)*	surprise
sucia, sucio *(SOO-syah, SOO-syoh)*	dirty
ti (a ti) *(TEE (ah TEE))*	you (to you)
tomates *(toh-MAH-tehs)*	tomatoes
torta *(TOHR-tah)*	cake
triste *(TREES-teh)*	sad

tu *(TOO)*	your
un, una, uno *(OON, OO-nah, OO-noh)*	one, a
un minuto *(OON mee-NOO-toh)*	just a minute
venir *(veh-NEER)*	come
viene *(VYEH-neh)*	(she/he) comes, is coming
y *(EE)*	and
yo *(YOH)*	I
zanahoria *(sah-nah-OH-ryah)*	carrot

LETTER TO LIBRARIANS, TEACHERS, AND PARENTS

Learning a new language can be intimidating. *Friends and Amigos* introduces a basic Spanish vocabulary in a challenging, yet familiar setting. New words are interspersed throughout each chapter and can be assimilated easily and naturally as young readers enjoy the story. The reinforcement that is so important in developing language skills is encouraged at the end of each chapter, where a list of words introduced in the previous pages offers pronunciation guides and basic definitions. *Friends and Amigos* also offers real-life stories that center around bilingual friendships, thus encouraging readers to recognize the tremendous value of cultural diversity in the world community.

The intriguing activities on page 76 help learning take place while having fun. Parents and teachers can incorporate many of these activities on a daily basis. The recommended books, videos, and web sites that follow on page 77 also help provide an enjoyable pathway to learning more about Spanish language and culture. These positive experiences will encourage young readers to explore a language other than their own.

ACTIVITIES

Famous people. Find the names of some famous Spanish-speaking people of today or from the past. Think about sports figures, musicians, people in public life, artists, and actors. Why are the persons you found famous? From what country did they come? Check the entry of a Spanish-speaking country in an encyclopedia or find a library book about the country for important people that may be listed. Ask a librarian, teacher, or parent to help you find this kind of information.

Similar words. Make a list of Spanish words that are similar to English, such as *tomates/tomatoes* and *sorpresa/surprise,* in *Happy Birthday, Anna, ¡Sorpresa!* Look in other books that have Spanish words and check through an English-Spanish dictionary. Make a game out of seeing which of your friends or classmates can write the longest list.

Map a country. Choose a Spanish-speaking country that seems interesting to you. Lay tracing paper over a map of this country. Trace the outline of the map carefully, then the major rivers, lakes, mountains, and other important features and label them. Label the capital city and other large cities. Color the map with crayons or color pencils. Draw the country's flag and color it.

MORE BOOKS TO READ

Argentina. Karen Jacobsen (Childrens Press)

Bolivia. Karen Schimmel (Chelsea House)

Diego Rivera. Mike Venezia (Childrens Press)

Mexico. Festivals of the World series. Elizabeth Berg (Gareth Stevens)

My Everyday Spanish Word Book. Michel Kahn (Barron)

Peru. Festivals of the World series. Leslie Jermyn (Gareth Stevens)

Puerto Rico. Festivals of the World series. Erin Foley (Gareth Stevens)

Simon Bolivar. (Raintree Steck-Vaughn)

VIDEOS

Felicidades, Perro Pepe: Perro Pepe's Birthday. (Agency for Instructional Technology)

Going Shopping. (Agency for Instructional Technology)

The Mexican Way of Life. (AIMS Media)

WEB SITES

www.nationalgeographic.com/resources/ngo/maps/atlas/samerica.html

www.nationalgeographic.com/resources/ngo/maps/atlas/namerica/namerica.html

Patricia Reilly Giff is the author of many fine books for children, including *The Kids of the Polk Street School* (series), *The Lincoln Lions Band* (series), *The Polka Dot Private Eye* (series), and *New Kids at the Polk Street School* (series). Ms. Giff received her bachelor's degree from Marymount College and a master's degree in history from St. John's University. She holds a Professional Diploma in Reading and a Doctorate of Humane Letters from Hofstra University. She was a teacher and reading consultant for many years. Ms. Giff lives in Weston, Connecticut.

DyAnne DiSalvo-Ryan has illustrated numerous books for children, including some she has written herself. She lives in Haddonfield, New Jersey.